Forew...

*I originally wrote this as a s... then revised it
as a book. The screenplay is available in film
on request.*

*This is a slightly revised version of my first book.
I hope you enjoy it.*

www.ericblyton.co.uk

CHAPTER ONE

Jim, the boy

L ate at night, the house was in silence, then all
of a sudden there was a thud from downstairs. Jane
nudged Philip. "Philip," she whispered, but nothing
happened, he was fast asleep. Again, a harder nudge.
"What is it?" said Philip. "I heard a noise
downstairs." Go and check it out, will you? Philip
rolled out of bed and felt around in the dark for his
slippers. "Quiet, shhh," said Jane. Philip replied,
"Why?" "It'll only be Jimmy, it always is, this is such
a waste of time." He opened the bedroom door,
walked down the staircase, and entered the lounge,
where he could see a light from the kitchen.

Philip walked quietly to the kitchen door. The light
was from the refrigerator, and standing there was
little Jimmy with a bottle of milk in his hand. Philip
watched from the door for a few moments as Jimmy
put the bottle back in the refrigerator and closed the
door. Jimmy then, without acknowledgment, walked

straight past Philip, went up the stairs, and went back to his bedroom.

Philip grabbed a glass and poured himself some water. Glass in hand, he headed up the stairs and walked into the bedroom, where Jane was sitting up in bed. "I told you so." "It was just Jimmy sleepwalking as usual," said Philip sarcastically. "Well, you never know, it might have been burglars or worse."

In the morning, the family was sitting around the table, Jane was cooking breakfast, Philip was reading his paper, and the boys, Jimmy and Peter, were poking and annoying each other quietly so as not to attract Philip's attention. Jane poured Philip a coffee. "Stop it, you two," she snapped at the boys. "He started it!" shouted Peter. "No, I didn't," defended Jimmy, and Philip looked over his paper at the boys and said, "I don't need to see what's going on to know who started it, do I, Peter?" "No, Dad," came the reply. "Just get your breakfast eaten and get ready for school," said Philip. "But I don't want to go to school! "I hate school!" Shouted Pete, angrily Philip responded, "You'll go to school whether you like it or not, my lad, why is it always you?" "We never get this sort of nonsense from Jimmy!" "Well, at least I don't wander around at night in a trance," retorted Pete. "Enough!" shouted Philip. "So Jimmy sleep walks, he'll grow out of that, but you!" "I really don't know where you get this attitude from, but you better change it, lad, or you won't have any sort of future, now get to school!"

Leaving his breakfast half eaten, Peter grabbed his school bag and stormed off, the front door could be heard slamming as he left.

Jimmy had sat quietly throughout the argument, then he spoke, "Dad, do I sleepwalk much?" "Yes, Jimmy, quite often," Jane interrupted as Philip resumed reading his paper. "What do I do when I sleepwalk?" asked Jimmy. "Oh, not much, you just do the things you do when you're awake, like get a drink, or sometimes nothing at all, just walk," she replied.

Jane ended the conversation with, "It really doesn't matter, Jimmy, like Dad said, it's something you'll grow out of when you're older." "Now off to school, there's a good boy."

Jimmy picked up his bag and headed for the door. "Bye, Mum, bye, Dad," he called as he left.

Philip put down his paper after folding it in half. He looked over to Jane and said, "What are we going to do about Peter?" "These boys are as alike as chalk and cheese, are you sure I'm Peter's father?" To which Jane replied, "What? Yes, of course you're his father, what do you take me for?" Philip smiled and said, "I know I am, where else would he, well, in fact, where do they get their devilish good looks from?" It's the devilish bad behaviour I'm more concerned about. Jimmy is the ideal child, obviously apart from the night adventures, but what about Peter? "Why does he hate everything and everyone?" " I really wish I knew Jane replied, "Just look at their school reports, Jimmy's are always good, but the schools

4

seem to write Pete up as some kind of thug." "I ask you, an eight-year-old thug, who the teachers are afraid of!"

Philip grumbled quietly and illegibly as he left the table and headed out to work.

Jimmy, standing alone in the school playground, was watching his brother play football with another boy's school bag when he was joined by Kyle.

"Why is Pete such a pig?" Asked Kyle, "I don't know, said Jimmy, but Dad's really angry at him right now, just look what he's doing to that bag," to which Kyle replied, "Yes, I know, it's mine, my Dad's going to go nuts when he sees it." Jimmy said, "Well, go and get it then." With a pained expression, Kyle looked down at his shoes and said, "I can't, he'll hit me."

"Can you get it?"

Just then, My Frazer, the geography teacher, rushed over, grabbed Peter by the collar, and with his other hand, picked up the bag, then frog marched the boy into the school building.

CHAPTER TWO
Twenty years later

Riley's Bar, an Irish-themed place but with a fifties or sixties feel about it, is always busy. At a table are a group of familiar faces, Jim and Kyle. Maggie and Joanne, these four, and Mike, who was sometimes there, were part and parcel of the fixtures and fittings, in fact, they were probably the most regular visitors to the bar with the exception of the staff.

The conversation was in full flow, as were the drinks. Riley's is always busy on a Friday night. Kyle turned to Jim and asked, "Jim, how's the love life?" Jim replied, "Ha!" What is love life, and how in hell am I supposed to have any sort of love life? "They keep changing my hours at work, and now they're talking about shift work!" Kyle said Come on, buddy, how long has it been since you dated anyone? Years? Jim protestingly responded, "No, not years, months admittedly, but certainly not years."

Maggie joined in, "Well, who was the last one, I mean the serious one, Jim?" "Jo, do you remember Jim's last girlfriend?" Joanne put on her thinking face and said, "Hmm, well, my memory is pretty good, but I can't remember that far back." Jim, still being defensive, tried to shut the conversation down with, "Oh, what is this?" Pick on Jim night?"

"Ok," said Kyle, "there are plenty of targets here, pick one!" "No," said Jim. "Alright," I'll pick one for you then," said Kyle. He then stood up, looked around, and marched off towards the bar where a woman in a blue dress sat nursing a drink alone. Kyle walked confidently up to her and started a conversation, within a minute he was back,

"Well? No joy?" Said Jim. Kyle thought carefully for a moment and then replied, "She's not your type Jim." Jim thought for a moment and then said, "Not your type?" "What exactly is my type, Kyle? She's probably out of my league, I mean, just look at her. She's stunning. Definitely one I would try for, so what's not "my type" about her?" Again Kyle chose his words carefully and responded with "maybe I should have said He's not your type"

Jim, in disbelief, said, "You mean?" Smiling Kyle replied, "Yes, she is a he."

At that moment Mike entered the bar, and when Mike entered anywhere he made an entrance shouting "Hiya Ladies!" loudly as he joined the group. Kyle argued the point of how they can all be ladies if two of them are men, but Mike ignored that, instead he was searching the room for possible targets. Kyle tapped him on the shoulder and said, "Mike, the girl in the blue dress at the end of the bar is alone and available." Mike being Mike immediately got up and headed across to the bar, straight up to the girl in the blue dress, and started pouring on the chat. When Mike was in chat-up mode, it was hard if not impossible to get a word in edgeways, and within a minute he was leaving the bar with the blue dress girl. Jim looked at Kyle, who was grinning from ear to ear, and said, "Kyle, is Mike?" But before he could finish the question, a very upset Mike re-appeared, heading across the floor. He sat down and said to Kyle, "You knew, didn't you?" Everyone burst into laughter. Maggie said, "Serves you right, ladies man!" To which Mike replied, "Yeah, yeah, but tell me, Kyle, how did you know?" Jim interrupted and said, "Because he tried to get her, him, anyway, tried to get me set up." Mike laughed and said, "I didn't think you swung both ways, Jimbo."

Jim stood up and said laughingly, "Well, I think you've tried to embarrass me enough tonight. I'm off home, I got an early start in the morning, and yes, I have to work on a Saturday. It's ok for you nine to five people, so I'll bid you adieu and see you all Wednesday night for the next instalment of humiliation." And with that, he left.

A few days later, Jim was doing some grocery shopping when he bumped into Mike. Mike was a bit flashy, he wore nice clothes, had ladies falling over themselves to be with him, had a nice car, and was a bit of a wheeler dealer. Jim was more than a little envious of him, so when the opportunity presented itself, he asked "Mike, what is your secret?" How do you do it? "You've got the lot, personality, money, style, come on, guy, what's the secret?"

Mike took Jim aside as if he were hiding the conversation from the other shoppers and said, "I wasn't always like this, you know, in fact, when I was younger, I was a bit nerdy, but then I met this guy, he got me into the golf club, and when I got to know him better, he did something that changed my life." Jim was now glued to this and said, "Tell me, Mike, go on, just spill it." So Mike said, "I don't know." "It was some kind of magic, hypnotherapy, or something else, I really don't know." Jim thought about this for about half a second before blurting, "I want some of that, do you still see this guy?" "Yes said Mike, "we play golf together every Sunday. Would you like an introduction?" Jim jumped at the chance, so Mike said he'd arrange it, and the two men went their separate ways.

It was Tuesday evening. Jim, Kyle, Maggie, and Joanne were at Jim's apartment playing truth or dare, which started off quite tamely but when the questions got a little more risqué, it was decided to switch to watching a movie instead. Jim was embarrassed because the questions had been more aimed at him and his love life, or lack thereof.

Jim and Joanne went to the kitchen to prepare some drinks and get some microwave popcorn on the go.

Maggie turned to Kyle and asked, "What is it with Jim?" "He never seems to try to meet anyone." Kyle replied, "I have no idea, maybe he's just shy, but he was seeing someone a while back, well, quite a while back, maybe he got hurt? I really don't know, he won't talk about it." Just then the drinks and popcorn arrived and the four friends settled down to watch TV. It was about twenty minutes into the movie when Jim's phone rang. He took it out to the kitchen to answer it. "Hello?" said Jim, and in an Indian accent he could hear a voice saying, "Hello my friend, I am Singeet, my good friend Michael has asked me to call you." Jim was stumped for a moment and then realised it was the guy he and Mike were talking about in the supermarket. "Oh, hi," said Jim. Singeet then went on to say, "Well, it is very nice to be talking with you. Michael says you are needing a little help with your life."

Jim was a little sceptical but interested enough to try whatever this was, after all, his life had been pretty dull for quite some time, and he was getting down, and unable to see a way out of his rut, he said, "Yes, I really could use a bit of luck." Singeet said, "Well, I am having to go to India on Friday, I can meet you at the airport drop-off zone at 3 p.m. if you are happy with that."

Jim agreed, he said he would be there, and went back to the lounge.

CHAPTER THREE

The happening

Friday came around, and Jim had been thinking about this meeting and wondering if he was doing the right thing, maybe it was just a waste of time. He'd had to arrange a shift change at work to accommodate this, and was debating whether or not to go, after all, he could be making a complete fool of himself. 2 p.m. came around, and at the last minute, Jim decided he had nothing to lose so he called a cab.

At the airport he saw a limo drawing up with Singy on the plate, the door opened and the chauffeur invited Jim to enter, once inside the limo Jim met Singeet, a very elderly Indian chap, complete with turban and incredibly long grey beard, Singeet presented a black bag just big enough to fit over Jim's face, Singeet said "What is it you desire my young friend?" Jim, still very doubtful, jokingly said, "To make my wildest dreams come true." Singeet asked if Jim was sure, and when Jim confirmed, Singeet said, "Ok, if you are sure, please place your face in the bag and be telling me what you are seeing." Jim hesitated for a moment and then thought why not, so he did as instructed. Jim said, "I can see a light, a bright white light, no wait, it's going pink, now red, yes, it's red." Singeet said, "Okay, very good, now please take the bag off your face, please."

Jim, in utter disbelief, said, "Is that it?" To which Singeet replied, "What were you expecting, my young friend, open surgery?" He said laughing loudly, Jim smiled, said goodbye and thanks, and then left the limo. As he was walking away, feeling exactly the same as he did when he arrived, Jim took a look over his shoulder only to see Singeet heading off with his bags into the terminal.

It was Wednesday, and once again the gang was at Riley's bar. Jim went to the gents, and as he walked in, he saw Mike washing his hands, who said, "Hey Jimbo, I wanted to get you alone, how did it go with Singeet?" Jim smiled, turned his head, and replied, "Funny, very funny." "Is this something you two cooked up between you to have a laugh at my expense?" Mike laughed. "No, honestly, what did you tell him you wanted out of life?" he said. Jim replied, "Obviously, I said I wanted my wildest dreams to come true." Mike looked worried. Jim saw this and said to Mike, "Why? What's wrong with that?" Mike looked away, a slight laugh in his voice as he replied quietly, "Nothing, Jimbo, nothing at all."

CHAPTER FOUR

Dream One

It was later that night. Jim had gotten himself all tucked up in his bed and drifted off to sleep. It was warm and comfortable, and Jim was having the most wonderful dream. He was an Arabian night, and one of the ladies from the sheik's harem had been giving him the eye, and Jim decided to follow this up. He knew if he got caught in the harem the sheikh would have his head on a spike, but she was so beautiful and he could no longer contain his desire, so he approached the harem, knew exactly which window to go to, climbed in quietly, and there before him was not one radiant beauty, but a whole room full of scantily dressed ladies in the finest silk nightwear. Jim's feet had barely touched the floor when they all rushed him, his shirt was off in under a second, his trousers were around his ankles, he was dragged into the middle of the room, these women were insatiable, Jim felt their hands all over his naked body, he could feel kisses everywhere, he was on his back, he felt the warm sensation as one of the beauties mounted him and began riding him hard like a horse racing across the desert, another was on his face, he could taste, umm, he thought for a moment he could taste uh? It was at that moment that Jim opened his eyes. It took a moment of realization, but then the horror of his situation became clear, he had been dreaming, yes, but he'd also been sleepwalking and climbed through the open window into the common room at the Cherry Hill residential home for elderly ladies. Jim pulled up his pyjama trousers, grabbed his pyjama top, and dove out through the open window head first. At that moment, Matron walked in to find all the old ladies giggling and adjusting their flannel nighties, all except Miss Jones, who'd slept through the whole thing.

"What's going on?" Snapped Matron, Iris trotted up to her and said, "We've all just had an orgy matron with a nice young man." "Nonsense!" said the matron, and after accusing them all of fantasizing, she left the room.

Meanwhile, Jim is running through the streets in a blind panic, horrified at what he had just done and thinking about what his friends would say if they knew or even what the police would do to him. He was looking for CCTV cameras or people out at this time, anything that could be used as evidence against him in court. He was also imagining life in prison and what the other inmates would do to him for such a crime. He finally arrived at his apartment, luckily, he hadn't locked up and was able to get inside. Jim rushed into the bathroom and into the shower, he scrubbed everywhere frantically with a brush until he was raw, he squirted toothpaste into his mouth directly from the tube and began brushing while pouring in mouthwash all at the same time, all the while trying to moan, "No, No, No, Oh my god, No!" through the torrent of soap, shampoo, toothpaste, and mouthwash.

In the morning, Jim was still sitting in the corner of the shower, he had not slept. His mind was racing, he thought about what if he'd been seen, what if the police had been called, the public humiliation, and how his friends would call him "Beast." How could he ever set foot outside the door again? After hours of worry, he began to realise that hiding wasn't going to solve anything, and sooner or later he would have to face the consequences, so Jim got dressed, and half expecting a lynch mob with burning torches to be waiting for him, he nervously left the building.

Outside, everything looked normal, the sun was shining, people were going about their daily business, and the black clouds and bolts of lightning were nowhere to be seen. Jim felt somewhat relieved, his relief increased as the day progressed, and normal life around him continued as if it were any other day.

CHAPTER FIVE

The Doctor

By mid-afternoon, Jim found himself on a park bench near the duck pond. He reached into his pocket and retrieved his phone, hesitantly dialled a number, and was greeted by the receptionist at his doctor's surgery. Jim wanted to make an appointment, but when the receptionist asked what the problem was, Jim froze, then said, "Er, um, it's... sleep walking." Then the question he was dreading, "What about it?" she asked, and Jim replied sternly, "It's personal, I'd rather discuss it with my doctor if you don't mind." Stern was not something Jim did easily. "Oh, ok. "If you want to be like that," said the receptionist, and she made him an appointment.

The following morning, Jim made his way to the doctor's office, checked in, sat down, and waited to be called. After what seemed like a lifetime spent on a hard chair in the waiting room, it was his turn. He entered the room and sat down. "What seems to be the problem, Jim?" asked Dr. Roberts. Jim explained what had happened, leaving out the bit where he's had sex with several old ladies, and asked if there was anything the doctor could do to help. "Unfortunately not," said Dr. Roberts. "You see, Jim, this is a mental problem, this is not my field at all." I can refer you to a specialist if you like. "Okay," said Jim, reluctantly. He was worried he may have to confess all the details, especially if this specialist hypnotised him. "Where will this be?" Asked Jim, "Oh, right here, I'll bring someone in," said Dr. Roberts, and with that, Jim left.

That night, Jim went to Riley's, Maggie was already there. Jim asked, "Hi Maggie, why is it you're always first here?" Maggie explained how she got there early so she could maybe pick up a guy before the rest of the gang arrived because they would only make fun of her. Jim asked her if she'd had any luck. "No," said Maggie, "but I always get bought a few drinks by guys with high hopes," she said laughing. "So why aren't you drunk before the rest of us?" he asked, so Maggie explained how she'd made an arrangement with the barman to add them to her tab so she could have them later. "Oh, clever," said Jim. "That's why you never buy a round then."

Just then, Joanne and Kyle arrived. Kyle offered to buy a round, then went to the bar. Joanne sat down with Jim and Maggie. "I went to see Gran today," said Joanne. Maggie asked, "How is she?" "She's good, you'll never guess what she told me happened the

19

other night," said Joanne, and then Joanne went on to describe the situation at the home.

Jim meanwhile was holding his breath, terrified he'd been identified as he had met Joanne's gran once, very briefly when he'd gone there with Joanne, it was a couple of years ago so maybe she didn't remember his face.

Joanne finished her story, and Jim choked as he finally began breathing again. "Are you ok?" inquired Kyle, who had just returned with the drinks. "Here, get this down your neck, Jim, it looks like you need it," said Kyle, handing Jim his drink.

The next morning, Jim went to the doctor's to meet this psychiatrist. He was sitting there talking to Dr. Roberts when a middle-aged woman in a tweed skirt suit entered, saying, "Hello, I'm Dr. Heggarty, I assume you're Jim?" She inquired. The three of them sat for a while as Jim explained, in graphic detail, about the sleepwalking, the orgies with the old folks, and even the meeting with Singeet.

Dr. Heggarty asked to be excused for a moment to confer with Dr. Roberts, and they left the room. From where Jim was sitting, he could hear talking on the other side of the door, it was too muffled to understand, but when the hysterical laughter began, he sort of got an idea of what was being said. The two doctors returned and sat down.

Dr. Heggarty turned to Jim and said, "I believe this is happening as a direct result of being hypnotized." Jim gave a sigh of relief. "So you can fix it? Yes? Just hypnotise me out of it," said Jim. Dr. Heggarty thought for a moment, looked briefly at Dr. Roberts, and said to Jim, "I'm sorry, Jim, but I can't." The only one who can undo this is the person who did it in the first place. He'll have a key word to get you out of it, you see."

Jim suddenly felt like his world had ended. "You mean I'm stuck with this? And it could happen again?" He asked. "Yes, I'm afraid so unless you can find this Mr. Singeet chap," said Dr. Heggarty, and with that, a rather dejected Jim left. A receptionist entered the room, and she closed the door behind him. As Jim walked away, he could hear all three of them laughing loudly.

As Jim walked home, he worried, "What if it happens again?" What could he do to prevent it? He thought. His self-esteem, was low. Jim hatched a plan. It wasn't going to be pleasant, but it was a plan. Jim phoned Kyle and asked him to pop round at about eight in the evening to collect Jim's keys and lock him inside his own apartment. He couldn't explain why, but they had been friends since childhood, so Kyle went along with it. The plan was for Kyle to return in the morning to let Jim out and give him his keys back. This would be every day, but at least it would ensure Jim didn't go back to the dreaded Merry Hill retirement home.

CHAPTER SIX

The Escape

T he plan seemed to be working until nearly a
week later, when Jim was asleep and having a very
realistic dream. He was a prisoner in Colditz Castle
during World War II, this may have had something to
do with the movie he'd watched on TV that evening,
and the fact he knew he was locked in. Jim was in his
cell, the guard was leaving, and as he locked the
heavy steel door, he said, "You will never escape, if
you do, you will be captured and shot!" A loud clunk
signalled the door was well and truly locked.

Jim, using the buckle of his belt, began scratching
around a flagstone in the floor, eventually, and with
great effort, it lifted. Below the stone was a plaster
ceiling, and Jim thought, "There must be a room
below here, if I can just break through, I can make my
escape." With that thought in mind, Jim jumped into
the hole he'd made, went crashing through the plaster,
and woke up as he landed in a full bath of water and

bubbles. Jim stood up, covered from head to toe in
bubbles, as the door swung open, and there stood a
beautiful young woman, a naked one, with a shocked
expression, her mouth open, looking first at Jim, then
at the ceiling, then at the door.

They both stood in silence looking at each other for a
second or two, but it felt to Jim like an eternity, then
Jim reached forward as if to shake hands. "Hi, I'm
Jim," he said, and immediately felt foolish. The
woman stood there, shocked and motionless. It took
several moments before Jim realized she was naked,
and then he handed her a towel that was hanging on a
rail by the bath, a towel that was obviously not big
enough to cover everything, but she did her best.

 Finally she spoke, she had been debating whether to
speak or just scream for help, but it was pretty
obvious this was the chap from upstairs who had
somehow managed to fall through to her bathroom.
"Hi," she said, "I'm Jenny." There was an awkward
silence, then again, stupidly, Jim blurted, "I'm from
upstairs!" "Really?" said Jenny. "I'd never have
guessed, but can you explain exactly what you're
doing in my bath?" Jim, realising he was still standing
in the bath, in which most of the water was now on
the floor, stepped out. Jenny stepped back. "Stop!"
she said. "Wait there, don't move." Jenny stepped
backward out of the bathroom door. A few moments
later, Jenny returned, wearing a bathrobe and carrying
towels, one of which she threw to Jim and the rest she
placed all over the wet floor. Jenny also threw a pair

of shorts and a T-shirt to Jim, "you better get dry and put these on," she said as she left the bathroom again. After a few minutes, Jim emerged from the bathroom to find Jenny sitting on the couch. She invited Jim to sit down and asked for an explanation. Jim explained about his sleepwalking and how he'd done it since childhood. He told her about Singeet and his dreams. He didn't mention the Merry Hill retirement home, as that was the most embarrassing event of his life.

By now, it was getting late, and Jim said he'd better be going. He promised to get the repairs done and headed for the door. As he left, he heard Jenny putting the door chain on and locking the door. Jim went up the stairs, and once at his door, he found he had no key, he remembered Kyle had his keys, so Jim, realising his phone was in his apartment, went outside to the payphone. It was raining heavily, so Jim made a run for it, the phone was at the end of the street, he arrived, already soaking wet, and felt for a pocket, then it dawned on him that he was still wearing Jenny's pink jogging shorts.

Jim got back to the foyer, luckily, the main door lock was broken, leaving him with no option. Jim thought if he could maybe climb back up through the hole in Jenny's ceiling, he could get into his place. He ran up the stairs, knocked on Jenny's door, and waited while she undid the vast array of locks, chains, and latches. Jenny peered through the gap in the chained door. "Oh my god, what do you want now?" she inquired. Jim explained, and reluctantly Jenny opened the door.

As Jim stepped inside, Jenny yelled, "Stop! "You're soaking wet again!" Jenny gave Jim another towel, and Jim, after drying himself, went to look at the bathroom ceiling. "There's no way I'll get through there, what can I do?" he said. Jenny thought for a moment and said, "You can use my phone to call your friend if you like."

"Great idea, but I just remembered that even if I had gotten change at the payphone, I still couldn't have called Kyle, his number is in my phone, and my phone is in my apartment," said Jim.

Jenny then said, "It looks like there's only one thing you can do then, you'll have to sleep on my couch tonight and get your keys in the morning, but not in those wet clothes." She then went off to her bedroom and returned wearing a skimpy lace nightdress. Jim thought his luck had changed, then she threw him the robe she had been wearing. "It's all I have that might fit you," she said.

Kyle arrived at the appointed time and found a note Jim had stuck on his door telling Kyle where he was. Kyle then went down the stairs and knocked on Jenny's door. After asking who was at the door, she let Kyle in, who was quite amused to see Jim there wearing an obviously too small bathrobe in Barby doll pink.

"What happened to you?" asked Kyle, laughing. Jim replied in a slightly grumpy tone, "I don't want to talk about it, the key thing isn't working, so you won't need to lock me up at night anymore." Kyle asked if Jim would be at Riley's later. Jim said he didn't know, he'd got quite a lot to sort out. Kyle left, and

Jenny locked up behind him. "Why so many locks?" asked Jim. Jenny hesitated, then said, "Maybe I'll tell you another time." Let's just say you were lucky to stay here last night. "I don't usually let men I don't know into my apartment in the first place." She laughed and then said, "I didn't get much of a choice with you, did I? You didn't use the door."

Jenny asked, "What are you going to do about this problem?" Jim thought for a moment, then said, "Mike! Mike knows him, he must know when he's coming back. I mean, they play golf together every week, so they must talk."

Jim said he would go to Riley's tonight as Mike often turns up. Jenny asked if she could come too. Jim agreed. "So it's a date then?" said Jim. Jenny reacted quickly, "No, don't go getting any ideas, I just want this resolved so I can get some peace and quiet!" Jim knew she wasn't being serious, she had a grin on her face while she said it.

That night at Riley's, the whole gang was there, including Mike, when Jim and Jenny arrived. They hadn't even sat down when Mike started the chat, and Jenny shot him down instantly, saying she'd heard about his reputation and to save his corny chat-up lines for the drunk ladies or transvestites. That did the trick, Mike was a little embarrassed that Jim had told her about the blue dress incident.

Jim saw Mike heading for the men's room, so he gave it a second or two, then followed him. Once inside, Jim asked Mike, "Hey Mike, when is your mate back from India?" Mike hesitated, then replied, "Why?" Jim explained about how his sleepwalking and his dreams had become a real problem, and he swore Mike to secrecy about the Merry Hill retirement home.

Mike finished washing his hands, and as he went to the dryer, Jim could see he was trying to refrain from laughing. "It's not funny, Mike! I could have gotten into some serious trouble." Mike replied, "Sounds like you already did, Jimbo," and burst into laughter. "I'm sorry," said Mike, "you've got to see the funny side of it, tell me, Jimbo, did they take their teeth out for a blo?" At that point, Jim shouted, "Stop it, Mike, for fuck's sake!" I'm having a crisis here, and you think it's funny! Just tell me when he's coming back from India!" " I have no idea when or even if he's coming back, Jimbo, but I will let you know if I see him. "In the meantime, keep me updated on your night-time adventures, will you?" said Mike, still laughing. Mike headed back to the others, and Jim followed shortly after. There was a bit of a chill in the air between Jim and Mike.

Jenny leaned towards Jim and quietly asked if he had the information he needed. Jim, still seething, replied through clenched teeth, "No, but Mike is being an arse."

 It wasn't long before Mike spotted a girl who appeared to be on her own. Joanne saw him looking and said, "Next victim, Mike?" Mike ignored her, got up, and headed across the room.

 "Something wrong?" asked Maggie. Jim turned towards her and asked, "Why?" Maggie had detected a bit of a rift between Jim and Mike. "Oh, it's just

Mike," said Jim, and Maggie said, "What is it? You know he's a predator." No, it's not that, it's personal," said Jim. Joanne joined the conversation, saying, "We're all friends here, you can share anything with us, you know that, Jim."
Jenny said Jim should tell them what's been going on, maybe someone might have a helpful suggestion, and so by the end of the evening everyone in the group knew what had been going on, obviously, Jim left out the graphic details of the Merry Hill saga.

CHAPTER SEVEN

The Alps

A few nights later about 7pm, Jim was in bed, he had an early shift the next day starting at the ungodly hour of 3am, he hadn't been asleep long and was dreaming he was the leader of a mountaineering expedition, he and his team were high up on a sheer cliff face, there was a blizzard raging, it was horrific, snow hitting like grit, the wind howling, all of a sudden the rope went tight, a member of the team had lost a footing and fallen, Jim grabbed him, he was battling to get the climber to a flat rock, Jim had hold of his coat and was dragging him with all his strength, the climber was screaming "Let me go!" save yourself,   Just let me go, Jim replied, shouting, "I won't leave anyone behind, hang on, we'll make it, not much further now." Again the screaming voice came back, only this time it was in a higher pitch, a woman's voice, "Let me go, you lunatic, let me go!" Somebody get this maniac off me!

At that moment, Jim opened his eyes to find himself in the shopping mall, dragging a screaming woman with bags of shopping up the escalator by her fur coat. He let go, which sent the woman rolling head over heels to the bottom of the escalator, collecting a few other people on the way. There was shopping flying everywhere. When she finally came to a stop, she was moving up the escalator feet first and face down. Someone hit the emergency button, which stopped it. Jim, meanwhile, was somewhat shocked when he saw two burly security guards heading down towards him. He panicked and jumped over the handrail onto the other side. Nearly at the bottom, there was a crowd of people tending to the bruised and battered woman.

Jim jumped over the rail and ran as fast as he could, wearing nothing but a pair of striped pajamas.

He arrived home. Gasping for breath, he reached his door, it was latched from the inside, and he had no pockets, so no keys.

There was only one thing for it, he thought, I'll have to go to Jenny's. Jim just needed to get out of public view, he imagined the entire police force combing the streets for him. He ran barefoot down the stairs and frantically banged on Jenny's door, "Who is it?" She called. Jim, who in a panic replied, "It's me, Jim, please open the door, Jenny, I need your help." Jenny undid all the locks, bolts, and chains, which seemed to take an eternity. Jim shot inside, turned on his heel, and started locking the door.

 "Whatever is the matter?" asked Jenny. Jim, still flustered, said, "I'm a fugitive, they're going to lock me up and throw away the key!" "I've done something awful!"

Jim sat down and explained it all to Jenny. She thought about it for a moment or two and said, "Well, it's not like you deliberately went out and robbed a bank or murdered anyone, is it? It probably won't even get reported." "I think you're worrying too much."

Jim felt a little better, so he called work to say he was sick and couldn't do the early shift. The truth was, he didn't have any clothes to wear, and a locksmith wouldn't be available at that hour, so it was another night on Jenny's couch. The two of them sat together, watching TV and drinking wine, as Jim didn't have to be away in the early hours after all.

The following evening, Jim and Kyle were at Riley's bar, Maggie was about somewhere too.

Kyle had seen her manipulating drinks out of some guy who wrongly thought his luck was in, the TV was on, and the local news was showing a cctv clip of some nutcase dragging a woman up the escalator at the shopping mall. The news reporter was saying how the woman had suffered minor injuries after the unknown assailant had forcibly and without provocation dragged her the majority of the way up the escalator, and the police were baffled.

Jim was cringing, his hands over his face, and ducking down over the bar. Kyle looked at the screen, then at Jim, and said, "Oh my god! " "That's you, Jim!" Jim said "Shhhh," and taking Kyle by the arm, he led him to a dimly lit table at the other end of the room.

Jim explained what had happened. Kyle didn't know whether to laugh or be serious, the whole thing looked hysterically funny, but he knew the repercussions would be serious if Jim was identified. Mike arrived, he strolled over to the table and greeted the friends with "Hi, Kyle" and a louder "Hiya celebrity!" Jim grabbed his arm and sat him down, and through gritted teeth, he said, "Mike! Shut up, will you? Have you any idea how much trouble I'd be in?" Mike then replied, "So it was you?" I thought so. "Another nightmare, eh?" "Never mind that," retorted Jim, "have you got any news on the Indian guy?" Mike said he hadn't, but again, Jim would be the first to know if he heard anything.

Jim sneaked out of Riley's, hoping no one recognised him from the news report. He went to Jenny's as it was safer, the police or Lynch mob wouldn't know where to find him.

Once the ritual unlocking and locking had been done, Jim asked Jenny about the bad experience that led to living in Fort Knox. She explained that she'd moved to the apartment to get away from her ex-boyfriend, who was controlling and violent. She was so scared she gave up her previous place and did a moonlight flit while he was away, but she was still afraid he may find her, thus the locks.

"Surely he couldn't be that bad?" Jim asked, and Jenny, who was obviously finding the conversation difficult, said, "He had a very short fuse, he would use his fists instead of his brain, and twice I ended up in the hospital." "That's terrible," said Jim. "I can't imagine having to live like that, you poor thing." Jenny was crying a little, and Jim put his arm around her, they were obviously getting closer, but Jenny had many barriers to get through.

"What time is work?" asked Jenny. Jim replied, "It isn't, I'm on the sick list at the moment, my doctor has signed me off with what he's calling depression and mental health issues."

Jenny asked if Jim would like to stay over, but Jim declined, saying there's no telling what he might get up to in his sleep, so it's best not to for the moment. Jenny was quite understanding.

Jim and Jenny were spending a lot of time together and not all through circumstance, Jim took her to the funfair that had just hit town, they laughed together, screamed together on the roller coaster, shared candy floss, they even went shopping together but not at the local shopping mall, Jim was still worried about being recognized.

CHAPTER EIGHT

The open air concert

It was Saturday morning. A hot, sunny day was inviting them both outside. Jenny had prepared a picnic, so off they went to the park. They laid out a blanket near the duck pond, arranged all the food, and set up a couple of sun loungers.

The park was very busy, there were families playing ball games, some boys had remote-control boats terrorising the ducks, and there was even a long queue at the ice cream van.
Jim and Jenny had eaten so much that Jim thought he was going to burst, so they settled down on the sun loungers to enjoy the heat.

Jenny sat up. "What's up?" inquired Jim. "Oh nothing, I just thought I recognised a voice," said Jenny, looking around. "Ah yes," she said, "it's Eric from work, I won't be long, do you want an ice cream?"

Jim said he'd love one, and with that, Jenny walked off, calling Eric! Eric was a colourful type, very slim, and wore 1970s styles, including huge flares on brightly coloured striped tight trousers and a brown suede waistcoat with a huge fur collar over a frilly shirt. Jenny caught up with him, and they talked as they made their way to the enormous line at the ice cream van.

It was quite some time before they got back to the picnic with ice creams in hand, and Jenny was wondering why there was such a huge crowd gathered there. As Jenny and Eric got closer, they heard bad singing. Someone was doing a one-man concert in the park and doing it so badly the crowd thought it was a comedy act and were laughing wildly.

Jenny made her way to the front and was amazed to see it was Jim, singing loudly into a half cucumber, and then he dived into the food on the picnic blanket, getting coleslaw, beetroot, salad cream, and a whole array of cold food all over his clothes.
The crowd was laughing hysterically as Jim went to stand up. Jenny dropped the ice cream and went to help him up. She shouted at the now dispersing crowd, "You should all be ashamed of yourselves!" "Can't you see he's not well?"

 Jenny introduced Jim to Eric, who then started to clean up. Eric, a little amused, said in a very camp way, "Oh, I have just got to hear this." Jenny sat Eric down and, while still packing the picnic away, explained what had been going on. Jim was keeping busy trying to hide his embarrassment while wiping the mayonnaise on his shirt, but in the process, he just spread it over a larger area.

Jenny asked Jim what had happened, and Jim explained, "I must have fallen asleep, I was dreaming I was a rock star and this was an open-air concert." "Oh, I see," said Jenny, "then what was the diving into the salad bowl all about?" Jim replied that he believed he was doing a stage dive and hitting the ground, and the pickle jar, which made hard contact with his ribs, was what woke him up.

Eric was now trying so hard to hold back the laughter that he had tears streaming down his face. He kept apologizing, and Jim said it was ok, it was a reaction he'd seen before and not to worry about it.

Jim was at home on Monday evening when there was a knock at the door. Jim opened the door to find his brother Pete standing there. "Hi Pete, come on in. A bit of an unexpected visit?" said Jim. Pete went inside and sat down while Jim made some coffee. Jim handed a cup to Pete and asked how he was and what he was doing there, as Pete was not one for socialising and often couldn't because from time to time he'd be in jail for one thing or another.

As the two men chatted about what life had held for them since they'd last seen each other some four years earlier, Jim asked, "Have you seen Mum and Dad?" Jim explained he was banned from the house, he had spoken to mum a few times on the phone and met up with her in town once, but dad wouldn't have anything to do with him. After a few hours of catching up, Pete said goodbye, and as he was leaving, he mentioned that he'd be around for a while and may pop around again if that's ok. Jim agreed.

Wednesday night saw the gang at Riley's, even Mike was there when Jim and Jenny arrived. Jenny sat down at the table while Jim went to the bar to get their drinks. When he approached the table, everyone was laughing but stopped as soon as they saw him. Jim sat down and passed Jenny her drink. "Ok, what's the joke?" Jim asked suspiciously. Mike chipped in, "Good gig, was it Jimbo?" Jim looked disapprovingly at Jenny and said, "You didn't, did you?" "No," she replied, so Jim asked, "Then how did you all know?" Jenny interrupted him, "Joanne knows Eric." Jim looked embarrassed. "Oh, great!" he said.
Mike was having a great time with this, he was doing Elvis impressions and telling jokes about stage dives and musicians until eventually Jim snapped, "It's all your fault in the first place, Mike." "Have you gotten hold of your mate yet?" Mike said he hadn't seen or heard from Singeet.

Once again, there was a tense atmosphere between Jim and Mike until a blonde in a mini skirt arrived and collected Mike.
"There he goes again, I really don't know how he does it," said Kyle. "Hopefully he'll catch something sore and painful," said Jim. Maggie responded, "Jim!

37

"You don't mean that, do you?" Jim said, "I suppose not, it's just that he's such a flash git and he's always taking the piss, even though he caused this mess!" Jenny said, "I'm sorry, Jim's a bit grumpy tonight, I'll take him home." "Understandable," said Maggie, and with that, Jenny and Jim left.

CHAPTER NINE
The family rift

Saturday morning Jim was at Jenny's where he'd stayed Friday night, they hadn't been up long when Jim's phone rang, it was Pete, he was at Jim's door, Jim explained he was one floor below and to come down, Jenny made an extra cup of coffee, and then came the knock at the door, Jim undid all of Jenny's locks and bolts, opened the door, and invited Pete in, Jenny emerged from the kitchen with a tray of coffee and biscuits, the moment she saw Pete she dropped the tray on the floor and screamed "What the hell "Get out, get out now, or I'm calling the police!" Pete stepped back out the door, Jim was on his heels, and no sooner were they out the door there was an almighty bang followed by Jenny securing all her locks.

"What was that?" asked Jim. Pete, still looking surprised, said, "Long story, bro." Jim knocked on the door. Jenny shouted, "Get lost!" How could you bring that monster to my home? I don't want to see you again! Jim stood silent. He could hear her crying through the door. He turned to Pete and said, "Right! Upstairs!   " You've got some explaining to do." They both went up to Jim's apartment, and all Pete could do was throw insults up about Jenny, how she was a lying bitch, it was her fault he got sent to jail, He told of how they were seeing each other and that she'd turned him in to the cops for robbing the bookies despite buying her gifts with the proceeds. Jim said, "But YOU robbed the bookies, not her, she did the decent thing, it's your fault you went to jail, not hers." Pete gave it the "whatever" attitude and told Jim to believe what he wants, "You're as bad as the old man!" Pete said.

Jim replied, "As bad as the old man?" He was right about you all along! "You're a waste of good air, now get out, you're no brother of mine!"
 Pete stormed off. Jim was furious, he sat there for a minute, then he heard shouting and banging from downstairs. Jim rushed down there to find Pete shouting and kicking Jenny's door. He rushed up to Pete and pushed him away from the door, yelling, "What do you think you're doing?"

Pete took a swing at Jim, but Jim stepped back. Pete charged at Jim, fists flying, he was in some rage! Again Jim avoided contact by side-stepping, Pete almost falling over, and again he went for Jim, but this time Jim hit him, a perfect shot, a right hander to Pete's jaw. Pete then grabbed Jim around the neck, and the two men were wrestling, kicking, and punching each other on the corridor floor. That's when the police arrived.

Philip went to the police station and spoke to the arresting officer. Jim could go without charge, he was told, but Pete was being charged because Jenny had previously taken an injunction out against him, and he'd broken that as well as the assault and a number of other offences the police had been wanting to ask Pete about. Philip was asked if he'd like to put up bail for Pete, but he declined, saying he could rot in there for all he cares.

Philip gave Jim a ride back to his apartment. "Well, when do I get to meet your young lady then?" said Philip. "To be honest, dad, I don't think she is anymore," said Jim. "Oh," said Philip sadly, "would you like me to talk to her for you, son?" Jim considered the offer for a moment and then said, "How would that look, dad?" "I'm a grown man having my dad do the talking for me. "I think I have to sort this out myself, but thanks for the offer."

Jim got out of Philip's car and walked slowly up the stairs. He thought about knocking on Jenny's door but decided to let the waters calm first.

Jim was sad. He sat down and switched on the TV. A few minutes later, the phone rang. It was Kyle, "Hi buddy, we're all at Riley's, are you coming?" he asked. Jim was in no mood for socializing, he just wanted to be alone. "Sorry, Kyle, not tonight. "I just got dumped thanks to Pete causing trouble, so I'm really not in the mood," said Jim. After a moment or two of silence, Kyle said, "You mean Jenny has finished with you?" "Of course, who else?" Jim replied sarcastically, and after a minute of sympathy and a "there are plenty more fish in the sea" speech from Kyle, Jim put his phone down, turned up the sound on the TV, and settled down to watch Pirates of the Caribbean.

The movie ended, so Jim tidied up and went to bed. He was soon asleep and having a great adventure, he was dreaming he was Captain Jack Sparrow, and his ship was in fierce battle, there were cannons blazing, masts falling, men dying, muskets firing, and then hand-to-hand fighting, Jim was shouting orders whilst fighting off the enemy, they were outnumbered and out-gunned, eventually Jim and his remaining crew were taken prisoner, and Jim was made to walk the plank, edging along slowly, while being prodded with a sword, Jim eventually got to the end, "That's odd," he thought, he could hear ducks, far out to sea! He held his nose and jumped. Then he hit the water—freezing-cold water. It took his breath away for a moment, then Jim opened his eyes and found himself sitting up to his neck in the duck pond! Mixed emotions ran through him, at least he wasn't doomed to drown in the middle of the ocean, but on the other hand, it was another rotten sleepwalk!

Now Jim was in a really bad mood, with sopping wet pajamas, squelching slippers, and mud in every orifice. Jim got home, and his door was wide open. This was good because he felt he really couldn't ask

Jenny for help, but bad because he could have been burgled, luckily he hadn't been. So Jim climbed into the shower while cursing Mike under his breath. He still blamed Mike because if it wasn't for him, Jim wouldn't be in this mess.

 After a few days of sulking and licking his wounds, Jim accepted his fate and went to Riley's Maggie and Kyle were there, Kyle was pretty much alone at the table because Maggie was off conning drinks out of various guys. "Hi Kyle," said Jim. "Jim, I never expected to see you here." I'm glad you are, as I've been abandoned." said Kyle.   Jim looked around, asking, "Where are the others?" He asked, at that moment Joanne appeared with Jenny. Jim thought about how the evening would go, there's bound to be an atmosphere between him and Jenny, but surprisingly, as the girls approached, Jenny put her arms around him and kissed him, "What's going on?" "Now I'm confused," said Jim. Jenny was about to answer when Joanne chipped in, "It's all sorted, Kyle and I went to Jenny's and explained all about Pete and that you had no idea about their history." Jim smiled, grabbed Jenny, and sat her on his knee.

 At the end of the evening, Jim and Jenny went to her apartment, sat down, and chatted. Jenny said she was looking for a new place, Jim asked why, and Jenny said it was because she was afraid Pete would return. Jim reassured her that Pete would never show his face again, but that wasn't enough.

"I have an idea," said Jim. "Let's get a place together." Jenny was a little shocked, they'd only just gotten back together, but she agreed, "You mean live together like husband and wife? She asked, "Yes, why not?"
Jenny smiled and jokingly asked, "Is that a proposal?"
"No," said Jim, "it's a practical arrangement." Would you excuse me just for a minute? I won't be long."
Jim ran upstairs and returned a minute or two later. Jenny was weighing up the "living arrangement" idea when Jim suddenly and without warning got down on one knee, produced the diamond ring he'd just fetched from upstairs, and taking Jenny's hand as the excitement welled up on her face, Jim said "This is a proposal" as he slid the ring on her finger and said "Will you marry me?"

  Jim and Jenny moved to a house in a village, it was idyllic, the wedding was held in the village church, obviously, Kyle was Jim's best man, Joanne cried all the way through the ceremony, and Maggie was telling everyone how she was never going to get married, it was the single life for her, but then she tried her hardest to catch the bouquet.

CHAPTER TEN
Golf

A few months passed, and Jim said he might take up golf. Jenny said, "But you always said it was a boring game for retired people with nothing more to do than hit a ball then go find it!"
"Well, there must be something in it because so many people do it," said Jim.

"How about I go and take a look?" "I can go through the woods and sit by the course and watch," Jim suggested. "Ok, that sounds like a plan," said Jenny.
By now, the sleepwalking was under control. Each night when they went to bed, they were handcuffed to each other, so if Jenny had to get up, she would take hers off and fix it to the bed, and if Jim had to get up, Jenny would go with him and stand by the door, a plan that seemed to work well right up until the Sunday when Jim was going to watch the golf.

The taxi dropped Jim off, and with a folding sun chair and sandwiches in hand, Jim walked through the woods to the edge of the golf course. He found a nice spot close to a bunker, so he set up his chair, put on his sunglasses, and chilled out while waiting for the action to start. An hour later, nothing had happened. Jim wondered if anyone was playing golf that day but decided to give it a bit longer.

Eventually Jim dropped off. Well, it was so warm and relaxing, and sleeping in handcuffs every night wasn't the most comfortable way to sleep, it was then that he started to dream.

It was World War II, Jim's patrol was pinned down at the edge of the woods, German artillery had gotten their position, they were being heavily shelled, Jim shouted, "We can't stay here, head for that bunker and dig in," A few soldiers made a run for it, one got hit as soon as they set off.

Jim and a couple of guys made it to the bunker, machine-gun fire was ringing out, they had no escape. Jim, shouting over the noise, asked, "Where's the radio?" "We need support, or we're all going to die here!" A voice replied, "Smithy's got it." Jim ordered, "Get Smithy up here now!" The soldier to Jim's left said, "He's dead, sir!" He got hit as we moved from the tree line! Jim thought for a second, then decided someone had to get the radio, he asked for a volunteer, no one wanted a suicide mission, Jim said, "I'll go, give me some covering fire!" He looked over the edge of the bunker—a crack! was heard in the distance, then a sharp pain to the side of Jim's head, and he was down!

Jim could hear voices, apart from the splitting headache, he thought he'd died and gone to heaven. "Is he dead?" asked one man, and in an Indian accent, the other replied, "Oh goodness gracious, I am hoping not." Jim thought he recognised the voice, opened his eyes, and standing over him holding a golf club was Singeet.

Jim sat up in amazement and said, "Singeet!" He yelled like he'd found a long-lost relative. "Thank God, I've been trying to find you for months!" said Jim excitedly. "Well, I have been playing golf every week, did Michael not tell you?" Jim thought for a moment and replied, "No, the horrible git told me you were still away in India."

Singeet said, "Oh no, no, no, my young friend, I have been back here since three days after I was seeing you at the airport." "I have been playing golf with Michael every week."

Jim explained to Singeet about the sleepwalking and what had happened, and Singeet said, "Come over here and look in this bag, what do you see?" Jim said "I see your golf clubs!" Singeet laughed and said, "I am only joking with you." I will remove your urge to walk when you sleep. "Listen carefully to my voice." Jim was listening carefully as Singeet spoke, then all of a sudden he awoke and asked, "Am I cured?" He asked"

"Yes, of course, all is well now," replied Singeet, and he went on to ask, "Why did Michael not tell you I had been here?"

Jim snapped, "Because he's a git, he thought the whole thing was funny, just wait until I get my hands on him!"
"Oh no, please do not be doing anything rash, my friend, you can leave Michael to me." Singeet smiled, he'd got something planned for Mike already.

CHAPTER ELEVEN

Payback

Another Wednesday night and the gang were at Riley's, Mike made his usual late but flamboyant entrance, Kyle went to tell him about Jim being cured, but Jim stopped him by interrupting, Mike asked, "How's life in dreamland, Jimbo?" Jim said "Oh you know, same same"

It wasn't long before Mike spotted a young lady on her own and trotted off to give her one of his famous chat-up lines. He was back within a few seconds with a red face where she'd slapped him, hard, Kyle laughing and asking Mike, "What was that?" "I don't know what happened," said Mike. "I went to ask her if she'd like a drink and heard myself saying my true intentions!" Kyle, trying not to laugh, asked, "What did you say to her?"

Mike replied, looking both confused and shocked, "I said, fancy a quick shag in the back seat of my motor?"

"It's no wonder she slapped you," said Maggie.
Mike was still in shock. "I don't understand it," he kept saying. "I've gone involuntarily honest and open!"
Jim was suppressing his delight, of course, he knew what it was all about. "Try again," he said. "Mike hesitated." Then, thinking he would say exactly what he had in mind, he went over to another girl and, meaning to say, "That's a lovely dress," suddenly blurted out, "Wow!" "Nice tits, can I get a feel?" Another slap!

When Mike returned to the table, he finally realised there was only one person who could have done this to him, "Singeet!" he said. Jim responded, "Yes, Mikey, Singeet, the guy you've been playing golf with all year, I was cursed with my sleepwalking nightmare for eleven months thanks to you, and oddly enough, that's how long Singeet is going to be in India for." Mike suddenly realised his predicament and said, "I'm not being stuck with this for nearly a year, when's he leaving?"
Jim replied, "Yesterday," and everyone burst into fits of laughter, except Mike.

Printed in Great Britain
by Amazon